Secrets of Disney's Glorious Gardens

KEVIN MARKEY

DISNEP
EDITIONS

NEW YORK

Special thanks to Jim Charlton, Robert Read, Maurice Ridore, Erin Blunt, Robert Carr, Les Frey, Teresa Prucha, Dave Smith, Jim Edgecomb, Fred Berning, Mike England, Tami Vais, Meg Fuchs, Angela Callahan, George Savvas, Cecile Eveland, Duncan Wardle, Donny Hall, Jamie Nielsen, and especially Janet Wyatt, and to everyone at Anderson's La Costa Nursery in La Costa, California, for their expertise, use of plants and facilities, and overall generosity, including: Una Tyler, Donna Coscia, Randee Guevara, Gabriella Fouse, Marsha Adams, and Andrea Akita.

For information address Disney Editions, 114 Fifth Avenue, New York, New York 10011-5690.
Editorial Director: Wendy Lefkon
Senior Editor: Jody Revenson

Library of Congress Cataloging-in-Publication Data on file.
Printed in Singapore
ISBN: 0-7868-5552-5
First Edition
10 9 8 7 6 5 4 3 2 1

zuppadesign

Designed and produced by Zuppa Design, P.O. Box 920519, Encinitas, California 92023-0519
Creative Directors: Kendra Haskins, Charles McStravick, and Monika Stout

contents

introduction

Disney Resorts are like life with a fresh coat of paint. They always seem just a little brighter, a little fresher, a little more colorful than the everyday world. The secret is not paint, however.

It is flowers.

From Fantasyland to Future World, Disneyland and Walt Disney World brim with flora. The Parks' magical gardens come in all shapes and sizes and play many roles. Some, such as the All-America Rose Selection Display Garden near the hub of Magic Kingdom Park at Walt Disney World, or the kaleidoscopic Victoria Gardens at Canada in Epcot's World Showcase, are attractions in their own right. Many more function as brilliant set designs, enhancing the exotic themes and evoking the far-off places of Disney's vast living stage. The seamless meshing of every detail may tempt visitors to take Disney's incredibly varied landscapes for granted. One wrong note, though, and the whole beautiful enterprise would suffer. Main Street, U.S.A., for instance, wouldn't be nearly so cheery without its vibrant hanging baskets.

Jungle Cruise without its jungles would be just another boat ride.

Disney's gardens serve practical purposes as well as imaginative ones. They bring shade to sunny California and Florida, screen private places from public ones, and create visual interest. The moods they generate are as varied as the flowers they contain, ranging from romantic to whimsical to nostalgic. In short, Disney's wondrous gardens accomplish what gardens everywhere do—only on a grander scale, for more people, and without an off-season.

Facts and figures hint at the vastness of Disney's gardens. Disneyland spreads across 160 acres, incorporating two distinct parks and eleven different lands, or areas. The Mickey Mouse floral parterre alone requires twenty-four thousand annuals a year. Even the grasses are impressive: the tiny lawns of Fantasyland's Storybook Land are planted with more than half a dozen different varieties, including Bermuda, blue sedge, dwarf reed,

Little Bunny Fountain grass, mondo grass, tufted hair grass, and zoysia.

Walt Disney World is even bigger, covering some four thousand acres of maintained landscapes and gardens. On these grow thirty-five hundred plant species—everything from common hothouse flowers to exotic specimens from every continent on Earth except Antarctica. Numbered among the collection are four million shrubs, some thirteen thousand roses (including more than one hundred different varieties at Epcot's famous rose walk alone), forty thousand ornamental trees, and scores of elaborate topiary sculptures, each one made up of as many as five hundred individual plants.

Perhaps the most impressive number of all is 650. That's how many professional horticulturists work to keep the gardens at Disneyland and Walt Disney World healthy and vivid. An eclectic and talented group, the horticultural staff includes arborists, irrigation specialists, bedding plant experts, orchid specialists, and pest management technicians. Each year at Walt Disney World, staffers artfully arrange more than three million annuals, nurture eighty-five hundred indoor plants, and produce four thousand brilliantly colored hanging baskets for display throughout the Magic Kingdom and other parks. They log 450,000 mower miles as they cut two thousand acres of turf, release 10.5 million beneficial insects to control plant pests, and experiment with hundreds of cultivars in an endless search for new and exciting plants.

Secrets of Disney's Glorious Gardens germinated in all that collective expertise.

Drawing on the experience of Disney's horticultural experts, the following pages serve as a hands-on guide as well as an armchair exploration of Disney's unforgettable landscapes. Packed with field-tested insights, growing tips, and ideas for Disney-style projects, the book aims to inspire as it explains. We hope it plants ideas that will help turn your own garden into a place of wonder and delight.

"PARTNERS"

"I THINK MOST OF ALL WHAT I WANT DISNEYLAND TO BE
IS A HAPPY PLACE, WHERE PARENTS AND CHILDREN
CAN HAVE FUN, TOGETHER."

Walt Disney

walt's idea blossoms

"I wanted something alive, something that could grow. Not only can I add things but even the trees will continue to grow. It will get more beautiful each year."

— WALT DISNEY ON DISNEYLAND

Walt Disney and Mickey Mouse greet guests of Disneyland. Walt wanted the park to appeal across generational lines to children, parents, and grandparents. With the help of landscape designer Morgan "Bill" Evans (above), he turned a patch of Southern California into the Happiest Place on Earth.

"Disneyland will never be completed," said Walt Disney at the Park's 1955 opening. "It will always continue to grow." Disney was talking about ideas and attractions, but he could have just as easily meant gardens and flowering trees. From the dense jungles of Adventureland to the tidy flower beds of Main Street, U.S.A., Disneyland's gardens have grown more vibrant and inventive each year. The lush gardens are the result of half a century of hard work and creativity, as horticulturists have applied every technique imaginable—even inventing new ones—to coax magic from the soil.

One of Walt's inspirations for Disneyland was Copenhagen's jewel-like Tivoli Gardens, a public park so lovely that littering seemed unthinkable. Walt wanted his own park to be such a place—clean and bursting with color. To execute his vision, he turned to landscape designer Morgan "Bill" Evans. A genius who almost single-handedly established the principles and practices of Disney landscape design, Evans would spend the next four decades refining Disneyland and every Disney park that followed.

"We landscaped all of Disneyland in less than a year with a maximum of arm-waving and a minimum of drawings," Evans once recalled. It was quite a feat. The project—a verdant central hub surrounded by five uniquely themed lands—was massive. It was also fraught with drama. With opening day fast approaching, the sandy earth underneath the Rivers of America waterway in Frontierland still drained like a sieve. Evans found the solution in a bed of local clay, which sealed the bottom as effectively as a swimming pool liner. The 2.5-acre tropical rain forest of Jungle Cruise in Adventureland posed its own challenges. Evans scoured the globe for exotic species that would thrive in Southern California, and also improvised with native plants. To achieve the look of gnarled jungle branches, he even planted orange trees upside down.

When the gates opened to the public, 160 acres of Anaheim orange groves had been transformed into the five realms of Disneyland, each with its own horticultural style. Not that everything was postcard perfect. After emptying

nurseries up and down California and running through his entire landscaping budget, Evans resorted to tagging weeds with Latin names to make them seem fancy.

Disneyland was such a success that ten years later, Walt Disney began acquiring land in Florida—twenty-seven thousand acres in all—to "build all the ideas and plans we can possibly imagine." Unfortunately, the site was mostly swampland and scrub forest, and required massive improvement before Walt Disney World could begin to take shape. To create a blank canvas for Evans and his crew, thousands of workers moved eight million cubic yards of soil and built fifty-five miles of levees and canals. They also shifted more than two thousand trees to new locations within the park. "The only thing I could think to do was get a lot of plants and see what took," Evans later said. He planted some sixty thousand flowers, shrubs, and trees, an effort that practically cleared out Florida nurseries and put a good dent in those of Alabama and Georgia.

At Disney World, Evans continued to cultivate the design principles that were first laid down in California and are practiced to this day. At the parks, the gardens function as part of the show, working with the architecture and other elements to tell a particular story. Landscapes must smoothly guide guests from one stage to the next, directing their attention to the attractions by minimizing off-screen distractions and intrusions. Finally, the gardens must be beautiful in their own right, delightful places that enhance both the parks and the pleasure guests find in them.

Minnie's House in Mickey's Toontown has the horticultural hallmarks of a country cottage, including hanging baskets and window boxes (above). Below (left to right): Walt Disney poses with an Audio-Animatronic rhino at Jungle Cruise; Bill Evans worked on every Disney theme park around the world, writing the book on landscaping as storytelling.

Before the day's guests arrive, Disneyland gardeners get to work. To keep gardens vibrant, all bedding plants are replaced with new ones every three months.

The Name Game

What's in a name? When it comes to flowers, quite a bit. Most casual gardeners know plants by their common names, such as forget-me-not or snapdragon. But in addition to these garden variety designations, all plants have dressier botanical names rendered in Latin. Officially, Forget-me-not is *Myosotis*, while snapdragon is *Antirrhinum majus*.

The first word denotes a plant's genus, while the second describes its species. Often a third Latin name is attached, which refers to a specific "cultivar" of the species— a "cultivated variety" or strain bred for specific qualities such as height, color, or hardiness. Common names are usually sufficient when buying plants, but in some cases, garden variety flowers go by several different names. For instance, bachelor's button (*Centaurea cyanus*) is also called cornflower.

It can be even more confusing when entirely different plants share a common name. Rose of Sharon, for example, also known as shrub althaea, is not a rose at all but a type of hibiscus (*Hibiscus syriacus*). Fortunately, botanical names refer to one plant only and they never vary—just one reason a smattering of Latin can be useful in the garden.

Landscape flourishes like a parterre garden and shrub animals extend the storybook magic of "it's a small world" to the grounds.

dramatic entrance

an easy-to-build entry arbor

Perfect as a gateway to your garden or a stand-alone accent, this traditional lattice-sided arbor can be built in a weekend by a couple of people with moderate carpentry skills.

MATERIALS:

(4) 10-foot-long 4 x 4 corner posts

(2) 5-foot-long 1 x 6 beams
(run side to side between tops of posts)

(5) 5-foot-long 1 x 6 end rafters
(run front-to-back between beams)

(Note: Use pressure-treated lumber, cedar, or redwood. After building the arbor, wait six months before staining.)

(2) 4-foot by 6-foot lattice panels

Wood screws

Jigsaw

3–4 bags of concrete

- Begin by notching each of the 4 corner posts to create housings for the roof beams. (Figure 1) Notches extend from the top end of the post 5.5 inches down the side. They should be 0.4 inches wide (the full width of the post) and 0.75 inches deep. Use a jigsaw to cut out the wood.

- Dig holes for the corner posts. Space each of the four holes 4 feet apart on center. Each hole should be about a foot in diameter and 3 feet deep.

- Place corner posts in the holes. Make sure tops point up, with notches facing out—forward on the two front posts, rearward on the back pair.

- Level and plumb the posts. To make sure the posts are the same height, lay a plank atop the front posts and place a carpenter's level on the plank. Repeat on the back posts and also from front to back. Make necessary adjustments. To check plumb, use a carpenter's level on all sides of the posts. Make necessary adjustments.

- Set posts with concrete. Mix concrete in a wheelbarrow and shovel it into the hole around the post, filling completely. (Figure 2)

- Repeat with remaining holes. Check that posts remain plumb. (Figure 3) It may help to temporarily brace posts with several pieces of scrap lumber. Allow the concrete to cure for one day.

- Attach front beam to forward posts. Position beam in notched housings on the posts; it will form a horizontal roofline across the tops of the posts. (Figure 4) Make sure the ends of the beam hang over the post equally—about 4 inches on either end. Fasten with wood screws.

- Attach rear beam. Again, position the beam horizontally so that it rests in the notches in the posts. Check overhangs. Screw in place.

- Attach end rafters. The end rafters run front to back, connecting the front posts to the back posts on either side of the arbor. Position them to the side faces of the corner posts, between the beams. Trim each one to fit (roughly 4 feet 4 inches), then screw the rafters to the posts.

- Attach three inside rafters, evenly spacing them about a foot apart. (Figure 5) Trim each rafter to fit, then fasten by screwing in place through the outside faces of the beams.

- Attach lattice side panels. (Figure 6) Position panels directly under end rafters on each side of the arbor and screw to post sides.

- Traditional arbor plants include wisteria, climbing roses, and grapevines. It will take several years for the vines to engulf the arbor, depending on climate, soil conditions, and other variables.

climate control

selecting the right plants for your region

In gardening, as in real estate, location matters. To take the guesswork out of finding plants that fit your climate, look no further than the United States Department of Agriculture's Plant Hardiness Zone Map. (You can check it out on the USDA Web site: www.usna.usda.gov/Hardzone/ushzmap.html)

Figure 1 Silverberry, Zone 2.   Figure 2 Japanese Bayberry, Zone 2.   Figure 3 Chinese Juniper, Zone 4.
Figure 4 Japanese Maple, Zone 6.   Figure 5 Strawberry Tree, Zone 8.

Figure 6 Fuchsia, Zone 9.
Figure 7 Bougainvillea, Zone 10

The map divides North America into ten different zones based on average annual low temperature. Zone 1, the coldest, covers parts of Canada, where minimum annual temperatures average a frosty -50 degrees F. Zone 10, the warmest, includes Hawaii and the southern tip of Florida, where annual minimum temperatures average above 40 degrees F. Excluding these arctic and tropical extremes, each zone represents a 10-degree gradation in average low temperature:

Zone 1: below -46° C (below -50° F)   Zone 6: -23° to -18° C (-10° to 0° F)

Zone 2: -46° to -40° C (-50° to -40° F)   Zone 7: -18° to -12° C (0° to 10° F)

Zone 3: -40° to -34° C (-40° to -30° F)   Zone 8: -12° to -7° C (10° to 20° F)

Zone 4: -34° to -29° C (-30° to -20° F)   Zone 9: -7° to -1° C (20° to 30° F)

Zone 5: -29° to -23° C (-20° to -10° F)   Zone 10: -1° to 4° C (30° to 40° F)

Largely determined by latitude and elevation, the zones band across the continent in a relatively consistent pattern. Significant differences can exist within small geographic areas, though. Compact Massachusetts contains four distinct rankings that range from Zone 7 (0 to 10 degrees F) along the mild southeastern coast to Zone 4 (-30 to -20 degrees F) in a frigid section of the Berkshire Hills to the west. The key to navigating your zone is simply finding the right plant and the right time to plant it. For instance, all Massachusetts green thumbs can have great success with columbines (generally able to withstand Zone 4 winters), but Cape Codders can sow them a lot earlier in the spring than their frostbitten neighbors.

Determining whether a plant will work for you is a simple two-step process. First, look up your location on the USDA map. Next, check plant tags, seed packages, and catalog descriptions to find the zone information. Plants listed as hardy to Zone 4, for example, can grow in Zones 10–4, but aren't cold resistant enough for Zones 3 and lower. Sometimes, the packaging will include a specific range, such as Zones 3–8, meaning that the plant is not suited to the heat at one end of the spectrum or the cold at the other. If plant and zone line up, you'll be in pretty good shape—at least as far as hardiness goes. Unfortunately, the map doesn't cover soil type, rainfall, heat, humidity, length of growing season, or sunlight and shade. To sort out these factors, there's no substitute for hands-on experience.

working large

trees for shade, privacy, and beauty

Trees can provide bold color, arresting fragrance, and elegant shape—all on a large scale. They complement architecture, offer shelter from sun and wind, and make appealing visual screens. When it comes to enhancing a theme or mood, trees have no rival—picture a romantic weeping mulberry, a tropical jacaranda, or an Old World stand of Italian cypress. For the gardener, no plant introduces more drama, dimension, or beauty to a landscape. Nurseries and county agricultural extensions can advise you on which trees are right for your climate and situation.

1

EVERGREEN SCREEN OR BORDER TREES:

Evergreen trees fall into two general categories. Broad-leafed evergreen, such as holly and live oak, have spreading branches and thick foliage. Coniferous evergreens, such as cedar, cypress, and pine, produce cones and have thinner leaves or needles. Disney's most famous evergreen is the massive Liberty Tree live oak in Liberty Square at Walt Disney World (Figure 1). At Grizzly Peak in Disneyland's California Adventure Park, sequoias and redwoods evoke the ruggedness of the Sierra Nevada Mountains. Popular evergreens include cedar, cypress, holly, live oak, eucalyptus, and spruce.

DECIDUOUS SHADE TREES:

Deciduous trees—those that shed foliage when the growing season ends—come in many sizes and shapes, with different textures and colors of leaves and bark. A stately oak is the very picture of strength, while a weeping willow or mulberry projects a softer, dreamier feel. The leaves of many deciduous species achieve vivid color before they drop, becoming the delight of the autumn landscape. Among prime Disney specimens are the smooth-barked sycamores that lend European charm to Epcot's Germany pavilion. Popular deciduous trees include ash, beech, birch, maple (Figure 2), oak, and willow.

FLOWERING TREES:

Flowering trees can be deciduous, such as cherry, or evergreen, such as magnolia. Disney resorts frequently use them to enhance an attraction's tropical ambience (Figure 3). Jungle Cruise at Disneyland features many breathtaking specimens, including a red-flowered South African coral tree. At Walt Disney World, beautiful golden-rain trees break out in spiky yellow flowers in the fall. After flowering, magnificent clusters of pink seedpods replace the sunny blossoms. Popular flowering trees include acacia, dogwood, cherry, crab apple, crape myrtle, jacaranda, Japanese pagoda, magnolia, mimosa (silk tree), and yellowwood.

2

3

PLANTING TIPS:

Most trees can be planted any time during the growing season, but generally they do best when planted in early spring or early fall. A spring planting gives them a chance to get acclimated before the growing season. A fall planting avoids stressful summer heat but allows them to settle in before cold weather arrives.

TIPS:

- Dig a hole 2 feet wider all around than the tree's root ball. (Figure 1)

- Fill the hole with water and let it stand overnight to check drainage. If water remains, either elevate the planting site by adding topsoil, choose a higher site, or improve drainage by digging a trench away and down from the hole and inserting a length of perforated pipe.

- Check soil quality: replace clay with topsoil; add loam to sandy earth. Break up soil chunks and remove rocks.

- Remove container-grown trees from planters. To encourage root growth, use a sharp knife to gently score the root ball of container-grown trees. Scores should be vertical and should be made every three inches all the way around the root ball. Be careful not to penetrate too deeply—$^1/_8$ inch is enough. On balled-and-burlapped trees, cut away plastic wrappings and cords. The burlap can be left in place.

- Place the root ball in the hole (Figure 2) and backfill about halfway, pressing the soil to eliminate pockets. Water thoroughly. After the water has soaked in, finish backfilling and use the leftover soil to build a berm around the tree. The berm should follow the outline of the hole and needn't be more than a few inches high (the amount of leftover soil will determine the height). Fill indentation with water. (Figure 3) Allow the water to soak in overnight, then fill again.

Disney introduced topiary figures to Disneyland in 1963. Scores of characters enliven the parks, today, including this frolicking pair at Walt Disney World.

lands of plenty

"Here is adventure. Here is romance. Here is mystery.
Tropical rivers silently flowing into the unknown.
The unbelievable splendor of exotic flowers."

— WALT DISNEY ON ADVENTURELAND

Left: Stonework, ferns, and a tranquil pool create a woodland ambience at Disneyland's Critter Country. Above: An antiqued statue set amid planters conjures the mystique of the Big Easy at New Orleans Square.

Variety. It's the spice of life and the seasoning that gives Disney's gardens their unique flavor. Like individual countries within continents, the lands of Disneyland and Walt Disney World each contain their own distinct personalities and physical characteristics. In differentiating them, Disney's horticultural themes achieve full flower.

At Disneyland, where Disney horticulturists and gardeners first perfected their art, miniature roses along Main Street, U.S.A., highlight a genteel sensibility. Nearby in Critter Country, thick, green blankets of ivy and fir trees give the park a wild, deeply forested look. New Orleans Square recalls the lush South with its potted cyclamen and chrysanthemums, whereas Frontierland's container gardens feature flowering herbs that hint at the land's pioneering spirit.

In Florida, the Magic Kingdom alone contains six environments diverse in color, style, and atmosphere. Like its California counterpart, Walt Disney World's Main Street, U.S.A., evokes turn-of-the-century, small-town America with formal Victorian gardens, manicured lawns, and shade trees. Soft pastels

Pink petunias and roses accentuate the graceful curves of a Walt Disney World pathway. The resort boasts some 13,000 rose plants.

flourish in the spring, when snapdragons rise above phlox and pansies in the flower beds. Bolder annuals such as begonias, salvia, and marigolds match summer's intensity, while bright chrysanthemums announce the arrival of fall. Meanwhile, baskets hanging from lampposts spill over with impatiens and geraniums, bringing splashes of color eye level.

Next door but a world apart lies tropical Adventureland. Here, the refinement of Main Street gives way to an exotic spectrum of flowering trees and shrubs. In place of elms and magnolias, palm trees, banyans, bamboo, and lacy fern trees abound. In this rain forest, home of the Jungle Cruise and the Swiss Family Tree House, bougainvillea, hibiscus, and cape honeysuckle blossom in a bold sunset of oranges, pinks, purples, and reds. Special techniques are required to make the illusions work. Cold-intolerant bougainvillea and Easter-lily vine, for example, are grown in huge containers hidden on the rooftops of attractions. When frost threatens—a rare but not unknown occurrence in Florida—cranes lower them to be stored in nursery greenhouses.

Recipe for Growth: A Walt Disney World Soil Mix

Good soil is essential to a healthy, attractive garden. This soil cocktail produces a nutrient-rich mixture that holds moisture, drains well, and uses pine bark and wood chips to foster plant-friendly microbes.

Mixture:

50% peat moss

10% green bark chips

40% sand

Mix in a large tub and use in planters or garden beds.

Just a short journey from lush Adventureland is Frontierland. The setting is the American Frontier, where the landscape ranges from hardwood forest to arid desert. Maples, sweetgums, oaks, sycamores, slash pines, and weeping willows provide an untamed backdrop for Tom Sawyer Island. Nearby, the landscape around Big Thunder Mountain Railroad captures the austere beauty of the Southwest with strategically planted yucca, jumping cactus, barrel cactus, prosopis, and prickly pear.

Fantasyland's colorful window boxes, stately hedges, and fanciful topiaries conjure the Europe of fairy tales. In a quaint village outside Cinderella's storybook castle, pink, red, and lavender annuals bloom festively in cottage gardens that display playful animals fashioned from yew. Shaggy, billowy deodar cedars, wobbling in the breeze like dancing bears, complete the whimsical picture.

Across the park in Tomorrowland, evergreens get much different treatment. Here, arborists shear Japanese yew into out-of-this-world clouds of foliage. Lifting off from boldly patterned beds of coleus, the effect is that of rockets blasting into space. Spiky, broad-leafed trees such as sago palm and Zamia reinforce the otherworldly look.

The final land within Walt Disney World's Magic Kingdom, Liberty Square, boasts the majestic Liberty Oak. Thirteen lanterns representing the original colonies adorn the 135-year-old southern live oak. The venerable

Top: Desert natives such as yucca, prickly pear, and barrel cactus contribute to the parched look of Frontierland's Big Thunder Mountain Railroad. Bottom (left to right): a ficus Simba sports a tufted mane of fiber-optic grass; colonial-style lanterns in Walt Disney World's magnificent Liberty Tree recall the midnight ride of Paul Revere.

oak was discovered on the property and moved to its present location in front of The Hall of Presidents during park construction. Standing forty feet high and weighing nearly forty tons, it remains one of the largest living specimens in all the parks. A blaze of red azaleas surrounds the enormous oak, while blue evolvulus and white impatiens in flower beds complete the colonial village's patriotic palette.

Another iconic American landscape can be seen at the resort's Disney-MGM Studios. Lined with towering Mexican fan palms, the main drag of Sunset Boulevard evokes the golden age of Hollywood and contemporary Beverly Hills.

At the far end of the avenue, The Twilight Zone Tower of Terror looms like an abandoned 1930s luxury hotel.

With overgrown azaleas, twisted oaks draped with Spanish moss, and thickets of bougainvillea, the neglected appearance of the grounds set the stage for the horrors within.

The landscaping of Epcot's Future World achieves the opposite effect. Beneath the gleaming dome of Spaceship Earth, dramatically pruned evergreens and precise geometric beds of annuals radiate order and vitality. Orange celosia, red salvia, and sunshine yellow calendula pop at every turn. Epcot's flower beds are sweeping, too: a single bed in front of The Land pavilion contains nearly thirty thousand plants. These Euclidian patterns, intense colors, and large numbers deliver a message that is as essential to Epcot as sweet nostalgia is to Main Street, U.S.A. "We have seen the future," the flora seems to shout, "and the future is bright."

During the 2005 Epcot International Flower Festival, a butterfly spreads its wings against a field of dusty miller in a Future World parterre.

a cut above

planting a productive cutting garden

Figure 1 Celosia. Figure 2 Shasta Daisy. Figure 3 Marigold. Figure 4 Coreopsis. Figure 5 Phlox.
Figure 6 Cosmos.

Cutting gardens are the gardens that keep on giving. They steadily provide flowers to enjoy indoors and out, and even generate new blooms after harvesting. A productive cutting garden has the same basic needs as an ornamental garden bed: organically rich soil that drains well, balanced fertilizer, water, and ample sunshine. Unlike formal beds, however, cutting gardens are planned for productivity rather than display. They're also likely to feature plants mismatched in color and shape. For this reason, many gardeners choose to plant them in discreet locations. There are no hard and fast rules, though. Depending on your personal taste and how aggressively you harvest, cutting gardens can be worked into display beds and borders.

PLANT SELECTION:

• Annuals bloom profusely and are the obvious choice for cutting gardens. The more you cut them, the more they grow.

• Long-blooming perennials such as black-eyed Susan, purple coneflower, and Shasta daisy also work well.

• Choose tall plants with long stems. They're easier to arrange in vases.

• For interesting bouquets, try growing different flower forms, such as spikes, balls, or trumpets.

GOOD CUTTING-GARDEN ANNUALS:

Calendula, celosia, centaurea (bachelor's button), cosmos, gypsophila (baby's breath; also available as a perennial), larkspur, marigold, salvia, snapdragon, zinnia

GOOD CUTTING-GARDEN PERENNIALS:

Achillea (yarrow), columbine, coreopsis, dianthus (pinks), delphinium, rudbeckia (coneflower), peony, phlox, Shasta daisy

GENERAL TIPS:

• Choose a flat and sunny spot that drains well.

• Plant flowers in 18-inch- to 36-inch-wide beds, oriented north to south.

• Plant tall flowers at the north end of the rows, so they don't shade shorter ones.

• Try incorporating a cutting garden into your vegetable garden. The combination is convenient—and colorful.

HARVESTING

• Cut blooms in the early morning, the coolest part of the day.

• Carry a water bucket while harvesting and immerse stems immediately.

• Trim stems before arranging in vase.

Figure 1 Dianthus. Figure 2 Salvia. Figure 3 Rudbeckia (coneflower). Figure 4 Gypsophila (baby's breath). Figure 5 Zinnia. Figure 6 Achillea (yarrow).

flower power

color, composition, and harmony in the garden

At the Disney Studio in California, animators use ink, paint, and computers to create movies that are works of art. The gardeners of Disney's resorts are also visual artists. Colorful plants are their paints, and the parks are their canvases. In effect, the resorts are carefully planned compositions. Using principles of color, composition, and harmony, you too can turn your landscape into a vivid work of art.

TIPS:

- Use color to frame focal points, such as statuary, large planters, or interesting shrubs and trees. (Figure 1) For example, set off an evergreen tree by planting a circular bed of bright red begonias around its trunk.

- Create visual interest with contrasting colors. (Figure 2)

- Use color to create mood and enhance themes. At Walt Disney World, the gardens of the wedding pavilion at the Grand Floridian Resort feature romantic white and pink roses (Figure 3), while the boldness of Epcot's Future World is underscored by a bright yellow and orange palette. In general terms, cool colors such as blue and soft violet instill serenity, while warm colors like yellow and red intensify emotion.

- Use symmetry to create formality. In the patriotic beds of Epcot's American Adventure, for instance, bands of red begonias and white impatiens form concentric circles around tall blue salvia to create a sense of order and strength.

3

- Create a high-impact rainbow effect by planting solid bands of plants in rows of different heights. (Figure 4) Alyssum, chrysanthemums, daffodils, impatiens, petunias, and zinnias can all work well to create blocks of color.

- Balance plantings by color, height, form, and weight. (Figure 5) A garden in which all the tall plants, for example, or all the cone-shaped ones are grouped together at one end will look as unsatisfying as a junior high school dance where all the boys hug the wall.

- Avoid "one-of-everything" gardens where dozens of different specimens are crammed into one plot. Too much variety destroys harmony. Instead, feature a few special plants, massing others to highlight the stars. (Figure 6)

- Bedding plants, hanging baskets, and containers can all be used to colorful effect. (Figure 7)

- Unify a flower bed by repeating a single element throughout—try bushy yellow buddleia, tall lilies, or homey daisies.

4

5

bold borders

creating effective edges

Whether in a suburban backyard or a Disney resort, creative border plantings can play many roles. They can help provide a transition from one area to another, create continuity by weaving different gardens together, and frame a bed or the edge of a yard, bringing order and definition to a landscape. Whatever the purpose, a strong border will help complete a picture.

TIPS:

- To achieve a mature-looking border quickly, eliminate gaps by planting densely. (Figure 1) Several tightly placed plants will grow to look like a single specimen.

- Simple isn't always better. Borders consisting of a solid block of color are powerful, but a subtle mix or a vibrant contrast of colors can also work. (Figure 2)

- Arrange borders containing several different plant types like you would a class picture: to ensure that all the plants get their day in the sun, low plants should go in the front row, medium ones behind them, and so on. (Figure 3)

- Use landscape features as backdrops to floral borders—brick walls, cedar fences, hedges, or shrubs are good choices. The interplay between a dark evergreen background and a colorful perennial border can be particularly striking.

- For an organic look, use borders to create curves in a landscape; for a formal appearance, plant borders in straight lines. (Figure 4)

- One size does not fit all. Depending on personal taste and the size and style of a garden, borders can be deep or shallow, low growing or relatively tall, and may consist of one kind of plant or several different types. (Figure 5)

- Many different annuals, bulbs, and perennials are suitable for borders. Some good ones include alyssum, chrysanthemum, cosmos, lavender, dianthus, marigolds, verbena, and zinnias.

Flower beds at Disneyland burst with vibrant colors.

setting a mood

"In those days it was all flat land—no rivers,
no mountains, no castles or rocket ships—just orange
groves and a few acres of walnut trees."
— WALT DISNEY ON DISNEYLAND

Left: In Italy at Epcot's
World Showcase,
terra-cotta container
gardens complement
the Old World stucco
and marble look of a
quiet piazza. Above:
Meticulously pruned,
a bonsai plant at Japan
in Epcot suggests an
ancient, weathered
tree.

Disney has as many moods as there are days in a year. In Epcot's France,
where it is always springtime, romance lingers among the Basque elms and
blooming crape myrtle trees. Japan projects an aura of quiet contemplation.
Patriotism blooms like an heirloom rose at the American Adventure. And the
nearby United Kingdom pavilion is as comfortably hospitable as a good cup of
tea. At the Polynesian Resort, a more languorous attitude prevails. A similar
atmosphere of serenity settles over the winding approach to Kali River Rapids
at Disney's Animal Kingdom. Meanwhile, an infectious sense of wonder perme-
ates Fantasyland. There, the pastel palette and the dancing elephant shrubs foster a feeling of childlike innocence—a marked contrast to the spooky sensation
that emanates from The Haunted Mansion in nearby Liberty Square.

Each mood is carefully orchestrated and comes with its own flower or
tree—or more likely, several hundred of each. Designed to enhance the theme of
an entire land or an individual attraction, Disney's gardens subtly encourage a
particular frame of mind.

Left: Begonias encircle a tree at Epcot's American Adventure. Annual beds at the attraction adhere to a red, white, and blue color scheme. Below: (left to right) Roses enhance the old-fashioned ambience of Main Street, U.S.A.; the tombstone of a family pig lurks in the shrubs at The Haunted Mansion; a sea serpent surfaces in Fantasyland.

In Disneyland's Fantasyland, playful animal topiaries prance amid plants and shrubs in front of It's a Small World. A second set of living sculptures heralds the antic spirit of Alice in Wonderland at the Lewis Carroll–inspired Mad Teacups attraction. Walt Disney World's Fantasyland takes the theme even further as Alice in Wonderland characters cavort atop a tea table carved from Japanese yew, paying homage to the zany book and its heroine's English pedigree.

Such pride of heritage drives the Epcot World Showcase American Adventure, where native trees—including American holly, eastern sycamore, magnolia, and Southern live oak—enliven the forecourt of an eighteenth-century Georgian-style mansion. Inside the building, key historic figures recount the formation of democracy in America.

Elsewhere in World Showcase, a floral palette of soft pink, yellow, lavender, and peach annuals gives the

France pavilion its special gaiety. Sycamore trees pleached in the European tradition, with top growth cut and side branches woven from tree to tree, form a delicate tracing of foliage that creates a year-round illusion of spring. An avenue of Basque elms completes the temporal enchantment. The garden in China nearby projects timelessness in a different sense. Corkscrew willow and weeping mulberry trees bow on the banks of a placid lily pond. Traditional Chinese stones complete the three-dimensional still life, projecting solidity and endurance.

Disney World's Animal Kingdom dedicates an entire section to Asia, with gardens and landscaping inspired by the flora and culture of India, Thailand, Tibet, and other countries. There, brilliant salmon, pink, and burgundy flowers of red silk-cotton trees infuse the area with energy. The showy pagoda flower, native to Southeast Asia, features spectacular pink and red blossoms that resemble tiered Chinese pagodas. The park's Bodhi Tree is also a nod to Asia's religious roots. Known as the "tree of awakening" in its native India, the tree—which can grow up to one hundred feet tall—is said to be the type under which Buddha gained enlightenment. Colorful cloth strips hang from the arching limbs of the magnificent specimen as a traditional sign of reverence. To glimpse the tree in all its glory is awe-inspiring.

Right: A serene landscape at the Japan pavilion in Epcot's World Showcase exalts the grandeur of nature by reflecting it on a small scale, a traditional concern of Japanese gardening. Carefully placed elements include water, symbolizing the sea, and rocks, representing the earth. A pagoda modeled after an eighth-century site in Japan rises behind a screen of Japanese cedar trees, evergreens that represent eternity.

The Asian tiger habitat in Disney's Animal Kingdom Park recalls
a ruined hunting lodge in India. The gnarled tree behind the
fountain is a Southern live oak.

Growing Tip: Poinsettias

Cheery poinsettias bloom in response to the shorter days of winter, making them a natural symbol of the holiday season. Native to Mexico, the plants were originally used by the Aztecs to stimulate circulation, treat skin infections, and fight fevers. In the 1820s, Joel Roberts Poinsett, the first U.S. ambassador to Mexico, introduced the plants to the United States. Upon Poinsett's death, Congress declared December 12 to be "National Poinsettia Day"—further popularizing the fiery winter plant.

For years, Disney's gardeners have used poinsettias to welcome the holidays by adorning the resorts' hanging baskets and signature towering poinsettia trees with thousands of the the bold red plants.

To brighten your own home or garden with these natural holiday ornaments, provide lots of indirect sunlight and somewhat humid conditions. Do not leave water resting on the leaves or bracts of the plant, though; doing so can cause a damaging fungus called botrytis. To remove droplets and dew from poinsettia leaves after watering, gently dry the plant with a handheld blower on a low setting.

Blood red and thorny, a tangle of roses engulfs a toppled bird bath outside the forbidding gates of The Haunted Mansion at Walt Disney World.

ghostly growth

a ghoulish garden inspired by The Haunted Mansion

Famously home to 999 grinning and ghoulish ghosts, The Haunted Mansion in Liberty Square harbors some unique life alongside its menagerie of the "undead." Plant life, that is. At Disneyland, the garden features black pansy, black mondo grass, blood leaf, and Medusa's head, contributing to the attraction's spooky appeal. To create your own haunted garden, try sowing some of these dark-blooming plants among your more traditional light-colored ones.

Against the somber backdrop of The Haunted Mansion, red roses create a funereal sensation (above).

PESTILENT PERENNIALS:

Daylily 'starling'—deep brown with golden throat

Sweet William 'sooty'—maroon

Lenten Rose 'little black'—near black

Iris 'superstition'—dark purple perennial

Tulips 'queen of night' and 'black parrot'—deep purple

AWFUL ANNUALS:

Cornflower 'black ball'—deep burgundy

Cosmos 'chocolate cosmos'—chocolate maroon

Geranium 'samobor'—green foliage with purplish circles

Pansy 'Molly Sanderson'—near black

Pincushion flower 'ace of spades'—dark purple

lemon fresh

a garden container

If life gives you lemon-scented plants, make a lemonade garden. You won't be able to drink it, but this fun theme garden will surround you with delightful fragrance. All you need is a large container, well-drained soil, and plenty of sun.

LEMON VERBENA:

Height: 18 inches

With its small white flowers and zesty fragrance, this plant looks as good as it smells. A South American native, it prefers full sun and light soil; it will not survive frost. Bring it indoors for winter in cold climates. The leaves can be dried and used to make potpourri or tea. (Figure 1)

LEMON BALM:

Height: 18 inches or more

A member of the mint family, this perennial bears small white-to-pale yellow and soft pink flowers throughout the summer. Its leaves are green and sweetly fragrant. The plant tolerates most types of soil and requires plenty of water. Herbalists prize lemon balm for its calming properties. (Figure 2)

LEMON THYME:

Height: 8 to 10 inches

A wonderfully aromatic perennial herb, lemon thyme requires light, well-drained soil and full sun. Its flowers are pale pinkish lilac. (Figure 3)

LEMON LILY: (not shown)
Height: 24 inches
A small daylily, the perennial Hemerocallis flava doesn't actually smell like citrus. The plant is named for its charming bright yellow flowers. Lemon lily does best in sun.

space is the place

a tomorrowland-inspired garden

The gardens of Tomorrowland use contrasting color schemes and geometric shapes to spin a futuristic fantasy. Boldly patterned annual beds create visual interest, while spiky, broad-leafed plants and trees like agaves, cycads, and palms provide a natural counterpoint to Tomorrowland's playful mod architecture. The park's signature plants, Japanese yews, are pruned into space-age puffs of foliage.

Futuristically pruned Japanese yew provide natural counterpoint to Tomorrowland's spires (above.)

Tomorrowland's landscaping, while bold, can be achieved at home on a smaller scale. Here are a few general guidelines to help send ordinary gardens into orbit.

TIPS:

- Embrace hot, vibrant color—for example, oranges, reds, and yellows. (Figure 1)

- Create patterns with big, bold-leafed plants. (Figure 2)

- Emphasize texture by juxtaposing different leaf forms, such as broad, spiky, or round. (Figure 3)

- Enhance contrasting colors by planting annuals in solid bands, such as racing stripes of red begonias and purple pentas. (Figure 4)

Walt Disney World's favorite futuristic plants:
- Large-leafed Traveler's palm
- Zamia and cycads
- Yuccas
- Dracaena

water works

cultivate serenity and color with a floating garden

Is anything so enchanting as a water garden? At the China pavilion, featuring a delightful mix of both Zen tranquility and high-energy impact, a flower-filled planter drifting in a body of water can transform any landscape.

MATERIALS:

4 sheets of polystyrene board, 2 inches thick and 36 inches wide

Latex base glue

Black acrylic interior/exterior spray paint

Florist knife

Sharp scissors

$1/4$-inch-thick capillary mat from a garden-supply store

Nylon cord and concrete block for anchors

4-inch eyebolt with nut and two 1-inch washers

Up to 50 4-inch bedding plants or one 1-gallon tropical plant and 20 4-inch plants

$1\frac{1}{2}$-cubic-foot light soil-less potting mix

Construction time: 2 to 4 hours

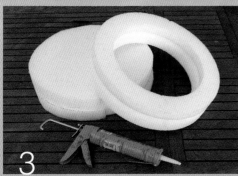

The good news for home gardeners is you don't need the vast spaces or extensive ponds of Walt Disney World to enjoy your own floating garden. Contrary to popular belief, water features are fairly easy to install and maintain. Many nurseries and garden-supply shops sell plastic pools. Once you've created your own pool or pond, follow the directions below to build and anchor a floating planter. Then fill it with whatever plants float your boat.

STEPS:

• Decide what size you want your planter to be. In this example, the planter has a diameter of 24 inches, which will accommodate about thirty-five plants. (Figure 1)

• Make a base for the planter by cutting two 24-inch diameter circles out of the 2-inch-thick polystyrene boards and gluing the circles together. (Figure 2)

• Cut two more 24-inch diameter circles from the remaining polystyrene boards. Then, leaving a 2-inch-wide rim, cut out the centers of the remaining two pieces. You will end up with two hollow circles, which will serve as the planter's walls. (Figure 3)

• Stack one hollowed-out section on top of the other and glue the pieces together. You now have a 4-inch-tall circular wall. Place it atop the base and glue in place.

• Drill four evenly spaced drain holes in the sides of the planter, one inch from the top. These will allow rainwater to escape. Now your planter is structurally complete. At this point, you may want to paint it black—white polystyrene tends to stick out in a natural landscape. (Figure 4)

- Line the bottom of the planter with capillary matting that is 24 inches in diameter. Then cut a 1-inch diameter hole through the center of the matting and bottom of the planter.

- Cut a strip of capillary matting 1 inch wide by 12 to 14 inches long to serve as a water wick. Insert the wick through the hole in the matting and planter bottom, allowing it to extend 8 to 10 inches below the bottom of the planter. Secure the wick by knotting it at the top, inside the planter. The wick will draw water into the planter, eliminating the need to wade into the pool to water the floating garden by hand. (Figure 5)

- Make an anchor for the planter. First drill another hole in the bottom of the planter, offset from the center. Next, fasten the 4-inch eyebolt, nut, and washer through the hole. Tie one end of a nylon cord to the eyebolt and tie the other end to the concrete block, making sure the cord is long enough for the planter to float when the block is resting at the bottom of the pool. The anchor will keep the container from drifting to the edge of your pool.

- Finish the planter by adding potting mix and plants. Depending on its size, your pool or pond may not get much shade. For this reason, sun-loving plants are recommended. Place the tallest plants in the center and cascading plants near the edges. (Figure 6, 7, 8)

The spiky fronds of a Bismarck palm and an arching live oak contribute
to an atmosphere of malign neglect at The Twilight Zone Tower of Terror
at Disney-MGM Studios.

international flora

A spine-covered floss silk tree pokes through the thick growth of the Mexico pavilion at Epcot. Native to Brazil, the species produces spectacular pink blooms in the fall. Tree-growing orchids (above) help complete the area's rain forest look.

In a sunny plaza of the Mexico pavilion at Epcot's World Showcase, an over 250-year-old double-spiked yucca grows beside a stucco wall. As one of the oldest living specimens at Walt Disney World, the ancient tree perfectly captures the timelessness of a desert market town. It's an eloquent botanic example of how landscape architects and gardeners recreate the look and feel of far flung places in Walt Disney World's two most international destinations, Epcot and Disney's Animal Kingdom. To tiptoe through the tulips—and olive groves and savanna grasses—of these parks is to take a trip around the world.

Each of the eleven pavilions in Epcot's World Showcase reflects a landscape as diverse as its culture, with distinct habitats often coexisting within a single land. At Mexico, for example, a dense tropical forest lies just a stone's throw from the arid yucca plaza. Here, fan palms, bougainvilleas, allamanda, and orchid-draped trees enclose a Mayan temple. A few countries away, vegetable plants and roses feature prominently in the gardens of Morocco. Both reflect the host country's agricultural traditions.

Architectural elements complement nature at Epcot's Japan Garden. From left to right: a winding footpath, a traditional stone lantern, and a symbolic rock "stream."

Wherever possible, designers use native plants to achieve their effects. Italy features a stand of gray-green olive trees. Native Japanese cedar, Japanese maple, and Japanese yew grace the refined landscape of the Japan Garden, where Bonsai shrubs, pastel azaleas, water, rocks, and a traditional arched footbridge all carry symbolic meaning. Chickasaw plum and citrus trees representing longevity and loyalty—the same ones that grow in the garden of Japan's Kyoto Palace—flank the pavilion's main building.

When conditions don't permit the use of native species, Disney's gardeners substitute botanical look-alikes. In Norway, delicate wildflowers sprout from traditional earthen roofs, as they do in the Norwegian countryside. A closer look, however, will prove they're not wildflowers at all, but Florida-friendly salvia, vinca, and impatiens that simply look the part. Meanwhile, what appears to be exotic

World View: Epcot International Flower and Garden Festival

Just around the time colder climate gardens burst into life each spring, hundreds of thousands of experts and amateurs from around the globe descend on Florida for Disney's world-famous Epcot International Flower and Garden Festival. Running from mid-April through the first week of June, the springtime tradition celebrates all things plant-related. Guests can check out innovative new garden designs; soak up daily presentations by notable guest speakers; pick up planting pointers at workshops by Disney horticulturists; exchange ideas with fellow enthusiasts; attend book signings; and simply revel in Epcot's award-winning gardens, which burst with some thirty million blossoms for the occasion.

Left: Yaupon holly forms an intricate border in the manicured Knot Garden of the United Kingdom in World Showcase. Each section of the kitchen-door plot is planted with different herbs, including chive, thyme, and parsley. Below (left to right): Earthy terra-cotta planters feature prominently in Epcot's Italy; a gravel-bottomed koi pond strikes a contemplative note in Japan; pink, white, and soft red flowers create a feeling of perpetual springtime in Paris at the France showcase.

tufted grass in China is actually zoysia turf allowed to grow unchecked. Next to the manicured Bermuda grass featured elsewhere in Epcot, it has the untamed look seen in traditional Chinese gardens.

In the France pavilion, horticulturists use pink-blooming crape myrtles—native to China and Korea but naturalized in the Southeast—to create the impression of perpetual springtime. The pavilion features a spectacular parterre, an ornamental garden that means "on the ground" in French. Shaped as a fleur-de-lis and patterned after French country embroidery, the parterre is one of Epcot's most famous gardens. It contains some three thousand impatiens, begonias, and other annuals, and is framed by a border hedge of yaupon holly. Designers chose the boxwood look-alike—once used by Native Americans as ipecac—because it stands up to Florida's subtropical climate. Yaupon also features prominently in the United Kingdom, bordering a knot garden or formal parterre

containing sections of oregano, basil, chive, thyme, and parsley.

Landscapes are bit wilder in Disney's Animal Kingdom, where the tidy annual beds of Epcot yield to the savannas, jungles, marshes, and bamboo groves of Asia and Africa. Sprawling five hundred lushly planted acres, Walt Disney World's largest park is home to some four million trees, ferns, grasses, plants, shrubs, and vines. No other Disney park in North America contains more flowering trees. Here, designers and gardeners use some of Disney's boldest specimens, including such native African species as baobabs, yellow acacias, and curious Kigelia africana. The latter, known as sausage trees, sport five-pound seed pods shaped like giant kielbasa links. To pollinate the trees, Disney horticulturists experimented with feather dusters and electric toothbrushes before discovering that birds did the trick nicely on their own.

Less visually striking but just as memorable are the Cananga odorata trees spread throughout The Oasis, a tropical garden at the entrance to Disney's Animal Kingdom. Native to the moist mountain valleys of Indo-Malaysia, the trees bear fragrant, delicate flowers. Traditionally, the blossoms are said to ward off evil spirits when soaked in coconut oil. Cananga odorata is also a main ingredient of the perfume Chanel No. 5. Visiting the park when these flowers are in bloom is like strolling through a French perfumery—just one more surprising and delightful destination on Disney's worldwide horticulture tour.

Above: The 145-foot-tall Tree of Life looks like a banyan but the man-made icon of Disney's Animal Kingdom actually houses a theater. It provides a majestic backdrop to flamingos wading in a marsh banked with elephant's ear plants. Below (left to right): A secluded courtyard along Maharajah Jungle Trek in Disney's Animal Kingdom; grasses weave a lush gorilla habitat in the Africa section of Disney's Animal Kingdom.

After the style of Norwegian country homes, an earth-covered roof of
Epcot's Norway pavilion supports what looks like a wildflower garden.
Close inspection reveals the plants as blue daze, vinca, and impatiens.

perennial powers

25 Popular Perennials

Figure 1 Achillea (yarrow). Figure 2 Rudbeckia (coneflower). Figure 3 Daylily. Figure 4 Periwinkle. Figure 5 Campanula. Figure 6 Dianthus.

Perennials survive year to year, unlike annuals, which die after one season of growth. Different perennials bloom at various times throughout the growing cycle—from early spring to late fall—making it possible to plant a garden that will always be in bloom. This ever-changing display can be a gardener's greatest joy.

ACHILLEA (YARROW)—Hardy to Zones 3–8. Easy-growing, drought-resistant yarrow does well in full sun and light, well-drained soil. Space plants twelve to eighteen inches apart. Divide every few years if flowers decrease in size. Blooming season: summer

ASTER—Hardy to Zones 5–6. Asters prefer moist, well-drained soil. Divide clumps every few years. Blooming season: fall

ASTILBE—Hardy to Zone 5. Astilbes need moist, somewhat acid soil and some shade. Divide in spring or fall. Blooming season: summer

BERGAMOT—Hardy to Zones 3–9, depending on hybrid. Bee balms do well in sun or partial shade and light, fertile, moist soil; they are prone to powdery mildew in dry conditions. Space new plants eighteen to twenty-four inches apart. Bee balms spread rapidly and, depending on garden size, may need to be weeded out every other year in the spring. Blooming season: summer

CAMPANULA (BELLFLOWER)—Hardy to Zones 2–5, depending on hybrid. Bellflowers thrive in moist, rich, well-drained soil with sun or partial shade. Tall varieties, such as grandiflora, can be cut back after flowering to encourage another bloom. Blooming season: early summer

CLEMATIS—Hardy to Zones 4–5. Provide clematis with loamy, moist soil and good drainage. They need sun or partial shade and prefer a warm climate. Plant clematis in the spring with manure and peat, digging holes at least one-foot deep. Fertilize young plants every six weeks during the growing season, and established ones twice a year. To promote a bushier vine, pinch the stems in the springtime. Support the vine on a trellis, arbor, fence, or other structure. Blooming season: early summer to fall

COLUMBINE—Hardy to Zones 4–5. Colorado's state flower prefers partial shade or full sun and well-drained soil. Columbines transplant easily when they are young and are also self-sowing. Blooming season: spring

COREOPSIS—Hardy to Zone 3. Coreopsis needs sun or partial shade but will grow in a variety of soil conditions. Blooming season: summer

DAYLILY—Hardy to Zones 3–4. Daylilies are tolerant of various conditions, but grow best in sun. They propagate relatively quickly. Blooming season: summer to early fall

DELPHINIUM—Hardy to Zones 3–4. Delphiniums prefer mild climates, alkaline soil, and sun. Protect them from wind by staking them to where the flower begins. Cut off the flowers when they are spent to encourage a second, late-summer bloom. Blooming season: early summer

DICENTRA (BLEEDING HEART)—Hardy to Zones 3–4. Bleeding hearts do well in partial shade and organically enriched, well-drained soil. Blooming season: spring to fall

DIANTHUS (PINKS)—Hardy to Zones 4–6. Pinks thrive in slightly alkaline soil with good drainage. Remove each bloom when spent to promote new flowering. Some hybrids should be divided every few years to keep them robust. Blooming season: first blooms are in the spring, then continue throughout the season

DIGITALIS (FOXGLOVE)—Hardy to Zone 5. Foxgloves require well-drained soil with rich organic content and partial shade. They are self-sowing, and spent flowers can be cut off to encourage rebloom. In colder climates, some foxgloves become unproductive after two years. Blooming season: early summer

ECHINACEA (PURPLE CONEFLOWER)—Hardy to Zone 4. Purple coneflowers will take full sun or partial shade and do well in most soils. Divide clumps every few years. Blooming season: late spring to fall

GERANIUM—Hardy to Zones 3–5, depending on the cultivar. Geraniums need moist, well-drained soil and prefer some shade in hot climates. Blooming season: late spring to midsummer

HIBISCUS—Hardy to Zones 4–8. Although hibiscus require lots of moisture, they need full sun and prefer a long, hot summer. Hibiscus tolerate most soils and will survive a cooler climate if the roots are mulched in winter. Blooming season: late summer and fall

IRIS—Hardy to Zones 4–5. Irises grow best in alkaline soil. Plant the roots with the tops visible to prevent rot and pest infestation. Blooming season: late spring

LIGULARIA (LEOPARD PLANT)—Hardy to Zones 4–8. Leopard plants are particular. They should be planted in the shade, but require partial sun. To thrive, they also need moist soil that does not dry out. Clay works well. Blooming season: mid to late summer

LUPINE—Hardy to Zone 5. Lupines need moist, acid, deep soil and sun or light shade. Fertilize after planting, then mulch to keep the roots cool. Blooming season: early summer

PEONY—Hardy to Zones 2–8. Peonies are adaptable to different conditions, but prefer deep, well-drained, organically rich soil and partial sun. For best results, plant to a maximum depth of two inches. Fertilize in early spring and after flowering. Finally, stake to keep heavy blooms from sagging. Blooming season: early summer and beyond

PERIWINKLE—Hardy to Zone 5. Periwinkle grows best in moist, slightly acid soil. The plants need sun and at least partial shade in hot climates. A low-lying ground cover, periwinkle grows to a height of just six inches and spreads by sending out runners, offshoots that put down their own roots. This new growth needs to be occasionally thinned or it may take over a garden. Blooming season: spring and summer

PHLOX—Hardy to Zones 4–5. Provide phlox with good drainage and organically enriched soil. To prevent mildew, allow space between plants to maximize air circulation. Blooming season: late spring and summer

PRIMROSE—Hardy to Zones 5–6. Plant primroses in moist, rich soil. They do well in partial shade and do not tolerate heat well. Divide them every second year after the flowers have bloomed. Blooming season: late spring and summer

RUDBECKIA (CONEFLOWER)—Hardy to Zone 3. These coneflowers accept different soil conditions and prefer full sun. Blooming season: summer

SHASTA DAISY—Hardy to Zones 4–5. Shasta daisies grow best in moist, well-drained soil. They need light shade in hot climates, but otherwise thrive in full sun. They are easy to divide. Blooming season: summer

TRILLIUM—Hardy to Zones 2–5, depending on species. Provide moist, organic, somewhat acid soil and mulch for trillium. Bulbs should be planted about two inches deep. They prefer partial shade when the weather heats up. Blooming season: spring and early summer

Figure 1 Clematis. Figure 2 Geranium. Figure 3 Echinacea (purple coneflower). Figure 4 Phlox. Figure 5 Hibiscus. Figure 6 Coreopsis.

keys to the cottage

Creating Your Own English Country Garden

Old-fashioned cottage-style gardens offer a beguiling alternative to formal designs. Densely packed with colorful blooms, refreshingly casual in appearance, and wildly eclectic, they exude a timeless romance irresistible to many flower lovers. Epcot's United Kingdom pavilion contains several captivating variations on the theme, including a perennial garden tucked beside Anne Hathaway's Cottage, a replica of the thatch-roofed home of William Shakespeare's wife.

English-style cottage gardens date back centuries to when families cultivated herbs, vegetables, and other useful plants in compact spaces just outside the front door. Today, almost anything goes in one of these unfettered landscapes. Flowering vines, annuals, perennials, herbs, vegetables, berries, bulbs, and shrubs can all contribute to the exuberant, free-flowing effect. Getting the natural look of a successful cottage garden takes some cultivation and savvy, though. And while there are no hard-and-fast design rules, a few basic principles can help.

containing the garden with a hedge, picket fence, or low stone wall sets it off from its surroundings so that it punctuates the landscape like an exclamation point.

Longevity—Cottage gardens should be lively, with something new growing all the time. The best ones are filled with plenty of long-blooming plants that give a colorful show throughout the season.

Variety—Forget refinement. Cottage gardens are meant to look wild, an effect achieved by including a myriad of plants. Mix perennials, vines, herbs, annuals, shrubs, or whatever strikes your fancy. Such variety acknowledges the practical history of the style and gives the gardens depth and texture.

A SIMPLE PLAN
Depending on your yard space, try designing your cottage garden either against the backdrop of a high wooden fence covered with flowering vines, along the side of a garage or garden shed, or around a trellis. In the latter case, rows can be planted as concentric circles around the vine trellis. For a free-flowing effect, allow the rows to wobble and intertwine a bit.

Compactness—Reflecting the practical nature of the earliest versions, an ideal cottage garden is compact. History aside, crowding the plants gives the style its profuse, almost overgrown quality. The dense growth also helps cut down on weeds.

Containment—Traditionally, cottage gardens needed enclosure to keep out foraging barnyard animals. Today,

home on the range

Using Ornamental Grasses

Ornamental grass can enhance any garden or landscape. Ranging in height from a few inches to more than fifteen feet, these grasses—commercially available in an ever-increasing number of species—are as versatile as they are lovely. Prized for their texture, shape, and color, they can be used to create unique backgrounds for perennial beds, as border plantings, for ground cover, and as delightful privacy screens. Many can be grown in containers as accent plants. Some stand up to both hot, dry summers and long, hard winters. They're relatively low-maintenance and resistant to disease and pests. Rustling in the breeze, grass enlivens a garden with sound and movement. No other plant is quite like it.

PLANT SELECTION

Choose cultivars hardy to your zone. Pay special attention to size—both spread and height. Some grasses bush out as they mature and will soon outgrow a narrow space. Others shoot up more than ten feet tall: you won't want to put them in front of a flower garden.

BED PREPARATION

Most grasses require ample sunshine. On the other hand, many will do fine in poor soil or clay, though it helps to give them a head start by turning over the bed and mixing in plenty of organic material. Tilling will encourage the plants to develop deep, healthy root systems.

PLANTING

Root growth slows down as the weather heats up, so the best time to plant is spring or early summer. Remove the grass from the pot and loosen the root ball. Dig a hole big enough to contain the root ball and fill the hole with water. Place the plant in the hole so that the ball is just above the surface and backfill with soil.

CARE AND MAINTENANCE

Follow watering recommendations for specific cultivars. Generally, ornamental grasses like moisture. In either fall or spring—many people like the subtle earth tones of winter grass—cut back old growth to a few inches, leaving a stubble ball. This is also a good time to fertilize with a 10-10-10 mixture. Like other clump-forming plants, certain grasses need to be divided every few years. Simply dig up the root ball, cut in half with a knife, and replant.

peace on earth

Japanese Gardens

Japanese gardens use ancient design principles and symbolic content to evoke the harmony of nature. Each stone, shrub, and water element is carefully placed to exist in balance with the others. Color palettes tend to be subtle, while open space is punctuated by clusters of curved plantings. Compared to Western formal gardens, with their precise geometry and profusion of color, delicately asymmetric Japanese gardens tend to reveal themselves slowly. For those willing to take the time, the reward can be a deep sense of serenity.

COMMON ELEMENTS:

STONES

More than plants, stones are the backbone of a Japanese garden. Broadly, they represent permanence, but individually, they can contain many secondary meanings. A single stone might serve as a simple sculptural element, or it could denote an entire mountain range. A curving line of flat stones can signify a rushing stream. Stepping-stones often connote passages through life, while the ever-changing surfaces of gravel gardens embody the sea and all it symbolizes—strength, vastness, eternity.

PLANTS

If stones suggest endurance, flowering plants in Japanese gardens symbolize change. As a result, trees and shrubs such as azalea, camellia, and cherry take precedence. Shrubs are arranged in groups of one, three, five, or seven, since odd numbers are traditionally considered lucky. Flowers are usually presented in solid blocks of color, with cheerful pastel hues punctuating the predominantly green landscape—exotic flowers are considered too showy. Other traditional plants include moss, bamboo, maple and pine trees. Long-growing pines carry a host of symbolic associations. Black pines are regarded as masculine and can represent the rugged coastal areas where they flourish. They are often pruned to suggest exposure to buffeting wind. Red or "feminine" pines, which are native to higher, inland regions, can be used to evoke mountain landscapes.

WATER

A vital garden component in the Japanese tradition, water symbolizes purity as well as the flowing nature of time. In addition to its symbolic purpose, water brings a delightful liveliness to the landscape. Typical expressions include stone drinking basins, surging waterfalls, trickling streams, and koi ponds. As with other elements in Japanese gardens, water features mimic nature by favoring graceful curves over straight lines and hard edges.

ORNAMENTS

Japanese gardens often contain architectural accents—most famously the traditional stone lanterns that are prized for their aged patina. Other common elements include fences and footbridges of natural cedar or bamboo, stone stupas, and water basins. Sometimes, accents are used to introduce the element of sound. Originally designed by farmers to startle foraging deer, the bamboo fountain or "deer scare" creates noise as its striking arm clacks against a well-placed stone. A spout at one end of the arm catches water from the trickling fountain; as the spout fills, the arm pivots under the weight in a see-saw like motion, spilling the water and causing the striking arm to fall rhythmically against a stone.

Potted flowers in many shades of pink and blue complement the Renaissance-style masonry of Epcot's Italy showcase.

trade secrets

"Our forests, waters, grasslands, and wildlife must be wisely used and protected."

— *WALT DISNEY ON CONSERVATION*

At the turn of the 19th century, train station gardens often spelled out the name of the town in flowers. The Magic Kingdom train station's giant Mickey Floral uses three thousand bedding plants to welcome guests to Walt Disney World.

In a kingdom as magical as Disney's, even the most colorful gardens occasionally need to be leavened by something more fantastic. To add enchantment, Disney's gardeners turn to horticultural specialties such as parterre gardens, topiary, and hanging baskets. These lively forms—modified for Disneyland and Walt Disney World and perfected by the horticulture staff—bring a heightened sense of wonder to the parks.

Since Disneyland's opening day in 1955, a smiling Mickey Mouse portrait-in-flowers has welcomed guests to the resort. Some six thousand color-coordinated annuals complete this spectacular "Mickey Floral" parterre. To create permanent displays such as this, Disney's gardeners begin by installing fiberglass header-board in the soil to form various components like ears, eyes, nose, mouth, and cheeks. Then the staff plants annuals of contrasting colors within each segment. When seen from above or afar, the result is stunning—like that of a living puzzle.

Other signature Disney parterres include the fleur-de-lis garden in Epcot's France pavilion and Walt Disney World's own Mickey Floral at the entrance to

the Magic Kingdom. The latter is perhaps the most photographed face on earth. More than a billion guests have visited Walt Disney World since it opened in 1971, and a good number have posed in front of the smiling mouse.

Like parterres, Disney-style topiaries also debuted at Disneyland. Inspired by the elaborate mazes and geometric-shaped shrubs he'd seen in Europe, Walt Disney asked his gardeners to create character-shaped shrubs for the resort. They obliged in 1963 with an evergreen Dumbo and other characters for Fantasyland. Today, both Disneyland and Walt Disney World display hundreds of forms, from the sheared trees of Tomorrowland to a menagerie of parading elephants, dancing hippos, slithering sea serpents, and larger-than-life Mickeys and Minnies.

To create such varied forms, Disney's gardeners practice several different styles of topiary. The oldest and most basic style, free form, consists of pruning trees and shrubs into unusual shapes, like cones, gumdrops, mazes, pyramids, and poodle puffs. Striking examples include the famous Dixie Cup Oaks of Walt Disney World's Contemporary Resort and the platform trees that ascend like stairways to heaven in front of Disneyland's It's a Small World.

The shrub topiary style uses metal frames to help shape shrubs into characters. Shrubs are planted in large wooden boxes at each point where the frame touches the ground. For instance, to create a giraffe for Disneyland's It's a Small World, Disney's horticulturists would use four shrubs— one for each foot. As the shrubs grow, gardeners trim

Goofy leads a parade of topiary characters at the Disneyland Nursery, a place known to insiders as the Chlorophyll Zoo. Below (left to right): A Fantasyland example of free-form topiary, one of several styles practiced by Disney; partially packed with sphagnum, a steel frame awaits only more moss and lots of fast-growing ficus to become an elephant.

them weekly until they completely engulf the frame. Depending on the size of the figure, the process can take three to ten years.

To speed things along, Disney's horticulturists perfected sphagnum topiary. Much faster to grow than shrub topiary and far more versatile than free form, this style allows gardeners to produce elaborate living sculptures in minimal time. To create sphagnum figures, Disney's artists first design a heavy steel frame to look like a specific character, such as Goofy or Simba from *The Lion King*. Gardeners then cover the frame with plastic mesh and pack it full of sphagnum moss. Next, they use an awl-like tool called a dibble to punch six to nine holes per square foot into the moss. Finally, they plug a fast-growing plant, such as English ivy or creeping fig, into each hole. Gardeners

trim and prune the plants until the foliage covers both the moss and the frame. To create effects like clothing or long hair, they contrast the vines with colorful plants like begonias and carnations, along with specialty grasses. Using the sphagnum technique, Disney's green-thumbed magicians can produce a mature topiary in as little as three months.

Horticulturists also use sphagnum to produce thousands of hanging baskets each year for Disneyland and Walt Disney World. Created for specific seasons and locations, these portable gardens add depth, texture, and color to virtually every corner of the parks. The sphagnum-style baskets accent Victorian architecture along Main Street, U.S.A., complement flower beds at Epcot, and enliven balconies and verandas at the resort hotels. When planted with exotic blends of foliage, they even

Ball-shaped hanging baskets provide voluminous color throughout
the parks. On any given day, close to a thousand baskets are displayed
at Walt Disney World.

reinforce the lush, tropical look of Adventureland.

Disney's hanging baskets feature an incredible range of annuals and perennials, including pansies, caladiums, impatiens, alyssum, verbena, lobelia, chrysanthemums, mandevilla, and petunias. Among the most charming sphagnum containers are the white and red poinsettia balls that dot the parks around the holidays. Each one contains about three dozen four-inch poinsettias. Cheery and bright, these hanging baskets are beacons of the season—and just one more example of how Disney's gardeners bring color and magic to the parks throughout the year.

Space to Grow

One commonly overlooked element of garden design is proper spacing. Because plants grow outward as well as upward, they need varying degrees of elbow room to achieve full flower. Optimal spacing not only gives plants leeway to soak up light, water, and soil nutrients, it also allows them to achieve a natural shape and cuts down on disease by allowing air to circulate.

Spacing Requirements for Some Common Annuals:

Begonia	Ten inches
Cosmos	Twelve inches or more
Geranium	Twelve to fifteen inches
Impatiens	Twelve inches
Marigold	Ten to eighteen inches
Pansy	Six to eight inches
Petunia	Ten to eighteen inches
Salvia	Twelve inches

Sphagnum topiary Bambi and friends peek between the blooms of lush Victoria Garden in the Canada showcase at Epcot.

picture perfect

Plants for Portraits

Disney's horticulturists use permanent forms called header boards and bender boards to define each flower bed within a parterre garden. Home gardeners, however, can create their own images on the ground using free form. In fact, depending on size and complexity, a home parterre can be created in just a few hours.

To make the best parterres, use compact, upright annuals with bright flowers. Tight growth keeps patterns consistent, while strong colors help define an image. Popular choices for annuals include alyssum, chrysanthemum, geranium, impatiens, Alternanthara, pansy, and wax begonia.

STEPS:

- Sketch a design on paper; in addition to size and shape, think about what colors you'll need. It may help to think of a parterre as a paint-by-numbers set, with flowers for paint. Popular designs include flags and names, but the possibilities are almost endless.

- Prepare the flower bed by turning over the soil, digging at least six inches down. Enrich the soil as needed by mixing peat, manure, and fertilizer.

- Level the surface of the bed with a rake.

- Trace the parterre design into the prepared bed and begin planting. For a ten-by-ten-foot garden, expect to use about two hundred plants spaced six inches apart.

basket case

How to Create a Disney-style Hanging Garden

Spilling over with colorful flowers and lush greenery, hanging baskets brighten every corner of the Walt Disney parks. Walt Disney World horticulturists produce some four thousand of the portable gardens every year. Each one takes about three months to cultivate in the backstage nursery. When they achieve full bloom, the baskets go "on-stage" in the parks, where they provide eye-level excitement, complement architecture, and enhance the themes of buildings and attractions.

As versatile as they are beautiful, Disney's signature basket gardens work with a wide range of annuals and can — and do — hang virtually anywhere, from lampposts to rafters to fences. At any given time Walt Disney World displays more than eight hundred baskets, their styles and colors as diverse as the resort itself. All-American red, white, and blue balls pump up the patriotism of Main Street U.S.A. Combinations of caladium, acalypha, and spider plants accentuate the exoticism of Adventureland. Masses of pink mandevilla make a splash in the Renaissance-style

plaza of Epcot's Italy pavilion. Disneyland's collection is equally broad and bright, ranging from the pretty petunia and primrose baskets that dress up the Central Plaza to the dazzling array of orchids and other exotics that spice up Adventureland's Enchanted Tiki Room. There's a hanging basket for every mood, location, and season.

Best of all for home gardeners, these eye-catching balls of color and personality are relatively easy to make. With proper care, a basket can last up to two years. Each one takes about an hour to plant.

Easy to make and maintain, hanging baskets enliven gardens and accent architecture by raising color to eye level. Various plants work well, including ivy geranium and vinca for cascading baskets, and begonias and impatiens for ball-shaped baskets.

MATERIALS:

Ten to fourteen-inch wire basket
Unmilled sphagnum moss
Potting soil
Twelve small plants
One tablespoon slow-release fertilizer
Gloves

TIPS:

• Wear gloves when working with sphagnum.

• Soak unmilled sphagnum until wet and squeeze out excess water.

• Sphagnum baskets can be either planted in the top — with the plants cascading over the sides — or in the top and sides to form a ball.

STEPS:

• Begin with an empty wire frame.

• Starting at bottom, firmly press sphagnum between wires; work your way up. (Figure 1)

• Completely stuff wires, then fill basket to within one inch of top with soil.

• If planting sides, poke holes in the sphagnum (Figure 2) and insert plants, tips even with the outside of the sphagnum. (Figure 3) Plant top and/or sides. (Figures 4 and 5)

• Add fertilizer; water well.

• Water daily when warm, fertilize weekly, and inspect for pests.

sculpture garden

Topiary Tips for Bringing Landscapes to Life

Topiary, the art of pruning and training living plants into ornamental shapes, falls in to three general categories: free form, shrub, and sphagnum. Each can be produced by amateur gardeners of varying degrees of experience, ambition, and patience.

FREE-FORM TOPIARY:

The oldest, simplest form of topiary requires only imagination—and a pair of sharp pruning shears—to change shrubs and trees into balls, squares, rectangles, and other geometric shapes. (Figures 1 and 2) Some tips for free form:

• Boxwood, holly, and Japanese yew work well for free-form topiary.

• Begin with sharp, well-oiled pruning shears.

• Prune hedges such as boxwood or holly so that they are broader at the bottom than the top.

• For straight lines, consider constructing a string guide line.

• After initial pruning, continue to trim and train until shrub or tree achieves desired shape, then practice routine maintenance. Growth time varies from a few weeks to months, depending on size and species.

• Fertilize regularly.

SHRUB TOPIARY:

Shrub topiary takes the longest to produce—up to ten years, depending on the type of shrub and the size of the frame. This style of topiary involves planting shrubs in large containers and growing them upward through and around metal frames designed to look like animals and other playful forms. (You can find these frames at select nurseries.) Some tips:

• Choose shrubs that shear well, are naturally full, and are fairly fast-growing; Japanese boxwood and Japanese yew are good choices.

• Fill a container with a well-drained soil mix.

Clockwise from left: A Mickey topiary of ficus and variegated ficus in progress at the Walt Disney World greenhouse. His pants may be finished in red begonia; a Chinese dragon rears his leafy head at Epcot World Showcase; animal shrub topiary complements the storybook facade of It's a Small World.

- Plant one shrub at each point where the frame touches the soil—two shrubs for the legs of Mickey Mouse, for example, four for Dumbo.

- After the shrubs are planted, place the frame over the plants

- Mulch and water.

- Clip, prune, and tie branches to encourage them to grow into the desired shape.

- Water and fertilize regularly.

- Maintain by shearing as needed.

TABLE TOP SPHAGNUM TOPIARY:

Sphagnum topiary are produced by stuffing a metal frame with moss and planting the sphagnum with close-growing vines. Widely available from garden centers and nurseries, tabletop metal topiary frames allow green thumbs to express their artistry, garnering quick and solid results. Some tips:

- Wear gloves when handling sphagnum moss.

- Cover the steel frame with plastic mesh, securing it with wire ties.

- Fill the frame with moistened unmilled sphagnum moss. Begin at the figure's extremities—hands, feet, tail, and so on.

- After filling the frame, tightly wrap the moss with fishing monofilament.

- Poke a hole in the sphagnum and plant small plants or plugs into the sphagnum. For faster coverage, plant several plugs. Creeping fig is a favorite.

- Pin vines into the moss with hair pins or fern pins.

- Water daily and fertilize regularly.

- Trim, pin, and prune weekly until the sphagnum is covered, then trim and pin as needed.

The Walt Disney World Nursery produces more than 10,000 hanging baskets every year. Each one is created for a specific site at the parks and resorts.

behind the scenes

"I certainly feel that trees are living, breathing individuals. They're alive and respond to the elements."

— *MORGAN "BILL" EVANS*

Left: A plug-sized plant of Alternanthera ready for planting at the Walt Disney World Nursery. The off-stage area features three greenhouses packed with annuals and specialty projects for the parks and resorts. Above: A Disney gardener at work.

How do Disney's gardens grow?

With hard work, imagination, and the coordinated efforts of a large group of dedicated experts.

By the time the gates open for the day and the first guests begin streaming into Disneyland and Walt Disney World, Disney's gardeners have already been at work for hours. A horticulturist's typical day begins at 5:00 a.m., when the resorts' gardeners, irrigation specialists, pest control technicians, gardeners, and tropical plant experts begin the daily chores necessary to care for the millions of plants on display. The arborists start even earlier. Because of the time-consuming nature of their work and the operational needs of the parks, arborists report for duty at 11:30 p.m. and work through the night, when they have Disney's veritable forest of trees all to themselves.

As the sun rises, crews of gardeners fan out to attend to the vast beds. Each team works in a specific area, deadheading old blooms, clearing gardens of fallen leaves, and pulling weeds. Much of the irrigation is taken care of automatically by a state-of-the-art computerized system, but there is always some supplemental

Behind the scenes, at least 1,500 hanging baskets are always in production for eventual display in the parks.

Decorative Art: Choosing Ornaments to Accent a Garden

Throughout the gardens of Walt Disney World and Disneyland, accents such as lighting fixtures, benches, wind chimes, statuary, and walkways complement the plants. A stone lantern greets guests at Epcot's Japan. Wrought iron lamps make a Colonial impression at Liberty Square in the Magic Kingdom. Colorful wooden birdhouses augment Splash Mountain's Song of the South theme.

The trick to successfully accenting a garden is choosing ornaments that suit the style, theme, and mood of your particular piece of earth. The right decorative element can complete a garden the way a rug, painting, or piece of furniture finishes a room. Conversely, the wrong one will stand out like a sore green thumb.

Terra-cotta pots add wonderful texture to the Old World flowering patios of Epcot's Italy showcase. Move the same planters over to rustic Canada, however, and they'd look about as out of place as a moose in St. Mark's square. The lesson: when it comes to garden ornaments, context is everything. Think about the effect you hope to create, then choose wisely.

watering to be done—and always before the park opens.

In a continuous effort to keep things fresh, each bedding plant is replaced seasonally. At Walt Disney World that adds up to three million plants four times a year, for a total of twelve million plantings. During these quarterly rotations, which can take up to a month to complete, gardeners begin work even earlier than usual, clocking in at 3:00 a.m. or even midnight. They dig with power augers until opening time, then switch to simple hand tools. Always, the safety and comfort of guests is of primary concern.

Over in Disney's Animal Kingdom, hundreds of orchids representing dozens of species adorn the trees in the rain forest–themed Oasis garden. There, orchid specialists stand on elevated platforms fastening tropical blooms with monofilament to various tree limbs to ensure a lively and constant display throughout the year. After a month to five weeks, the orchids root themselves to the trees, where they grow without soil. Once the graft is complete, the ties are cut away. Ideally, Disney specialists like to finish this part of the work before the gates open. Given the vagaries of gardening, however, that isn't always possible. This has led guests to remark at the strange sight of Disney's "tree surgeons, sewing flowers into the branches."

Meanwhile, other horticulturists work behind the scenes in nurseries, greenhouses, and trial gardens. The greenhouses contain thousands of plants—everything from annuals awaiting placement in park beds, to prized orchids, to rare and

Left: Orchids are fastened to trees with monofilament in Mexico at Epcot World Showcase. Other tricks of the trade employed by Disney's orchid specialists: the discrete use of space heaters to warm the tropical beauties when temperatures dip low. Opposite (left to right): Nursery annuals earmarked for Fantasyland; a pumpkin grown in the shape of Mickey at Epcot's Living With the Land experimental nursery; exotic grass topiary under construction.

Right: The All-America Selections Trial Grounds at the Walt Disney World Nursery. Southernmost of 41 AAS-certified gardens across the United States and Canada, the trial garden grows upwards of 500 annuals at any one time, testing them for hardiness, disease resistance, bloom quality, and uniformity of height and color. Cultivars passing muster end up in your local garden center — and possibly on display in the parks.

exotic plants. One such specimen is the unusual Titan arum, otherwise known as the Sumatra corpse flower. During its forty-year lifespan, the twelve-foot-tall Titan may bloom only two or three times, producing a single enormous bloom that lasts just one day and reeks of rotting meat.

Far sweeter-smelling are the five hundred or so plants growing in Disney's trial gardens. There, gardeners test new cultivars for suitability in the parks, monitoring characteristics such as how they stand up to the local climate and whether they bloom sporadically or in unison. Horticulturists also consider if the plants must be deadheaded by hand or whether they incise their blooms themselves. Plants may even be tested to determine how frequently they need water. Hybrids that perform well stand a good chance of being planted into gardens around the resort. Whether common or exotic, Disney's horticulturists are always looking for new plants to keep the gardens beautiful and fresh.

After careful cultivation in the Nursery, cartloads of annuals are ready for planting at Disneyland. A fresh batch will soon take their place.

taking wing

How to Attract Butterflies

Designing a garden to lure butterflies can be a delightful way to help your landscape come alive. North America is home to more than seven hundred species of these delicate creatures, and no two species prefer exactly the same plants. But a few general guidelines can go a long way toward creating a butterfly-friendly environment. Best of all, a bright, long-blooming, color-coordinated butterfly garden is lovely in its own right.

Florida is home to more than 100 butterfly species, many of which have been known to drop by the Wildlife Garden at Epcot.

Figure 1 Plumbago. Figure 2 Star Cluster (Pentas). Figure 3 Rudbeckia (Coneflower). Figure 4 Dianthus. Figure 5 Phlox. Figure 6 Butterfly Bush (Buddleia).

Figure 1 Mallow. Figure 2 Bee Balm. Figure 3 Verbena Bonariensis. Figure 4 Coreopsis.

TIPS:

- Plant your butterfly garden in the sun. Butterflies gain energy from light, and the plants that attract them generally thrive in sunshine.

- Include lots of flowers that produce nectar, an essential nourishment for butterflies. Caterpillars need nourishment, too. They feed on plants known as larval plants. Some examples include apple, cherry, and citrus trees; hosta; milkweed; passion vine; and snapdragons.

- Plant flowers that will bloom throughout the growing season. Butterflies are active from spring to fall, so ideally your garden should be, too.

- Group your plants to create swaths of color. Butterflies are attracted to plants first by hue, and they can see a large splash of color more readily than a single dot of color.

- Create damp areas and shallow puddles that invite butterflies to drink.

- Add a few flat stones as perches where butterflies can bask in the sun.

- Grow vines on a fence to create overnight roosting areas. A screen of shrubs can also provide shelter from weather and wind.

- Avoid pesticides, most of which are indiscriminately toxic to butterflies as well as garden pests. If insects are a problem, try horticultural soaps or oils instead.

GOOD BUTTERFLY FLOWERS:

acanthus	milkweed
bee balm	nasturtium
butterfly bush (buddleia)	phlox
chickweed	plumbago
coneflower	star cluster
coreopsis	Shrub verbena
dianthus	Queen Anne's lace
honeysuckle	thistle
mallow	wisteria

good riddance
Methods of Organic Pest Control

Whenever possible, Disney's horticulture team avoids using chemical pesticides. Instead, for more than a decade, horticulturists have practiced integrated pest management (IPM), a gardening method that uses beneficial insects—yes, some insects can actually improve a garden—and environmentally safe soaps and oils to control unwelcome marauders. There are many types of beneficial bugs. For example, the predatory beetle, *Delphastus puslius*, can eat up to five hundred whitefly eggs each day—pests that would otherwise devour plants. Other beneficial insects include lacewings, ladybugs (Figure 1), minute pirate bugs, meal (or "potato") bugs, and predator wasps, which don't sting but do devour aphids.

1

Birds also are rapacious eaters of insects. To attract these natural predators, place bird feeders and berry-bearing plants throughout your garden (Figure 2). If these methods don't work, try plant-derived compounds such as pyrethrum and rotenone. Effective and biodegradable, such compounds won't leave behind toxic residue, unlike conventional pesticides.

Experiment to find out what will work in your garden. Before automatically turning to the nearest can of pesticide, try some techniques of integrated pest management. The right combination can produce a clean, healthy garden.

GREEN PEST-CONTROL TIPS:

- Rake up leaves and clippings that can harbor pests.

- Regularly inspect your garden for invasions and remove any pests by hand.

- Cultivate plants that attract good bugs to your garden. Cosmos, dill, fennel, and yarrow appeal to lacewings; butterfly weed, marigold, and tansy attract ladybugs; and alfalfa, spearmint, and goldenrod—yes, goldenrod—are favored by minute pirate bugs. The good and bad bugs will find a natural balance in a healthy garden.

- If your pest population booms, use horticultural soaps and oils to minimize the intruders. You can make your own simple mixture and apply it with a clean spray bottle. Mix one tablespoon of a mild citrus dishwashing liquid and one tablespoon of cooking oil in a quart of water. This solution will take care of the soft-bodied pests and not harm the slightly harder beneficials.

EFFECTIVE INSPECTION

Inspecting your integrated pest management (IPM) garden is key to maintaining an adequate level of good bugs. While you're at it, you'll learn a good deal about your plants and the insects they harbor.

- Thoroughly inspect your garden at least once a week

- Take the time to walk through all of your plants

- While inspecting, turn over leaves and occasionally get down on your hands and knees to see who has moved in, who is still here, and who has moved out

- A healthy garden will almost always have small populations of pest insects — the bad bugs are what draw the good bugs in.

2

expert tips
Caring for Roses

Visitors to the Disney parks have no need for rose-colored glasses. Why? Delicate, fragrant roses already abound throughout Walt Disney World and Disneyland, accenting architecture, generating romance, and creating a feast for the eyes. More than ten thousand rose bushes of some three dozen varieties are on display at Walt Disney World (Figure 1). Highlights include the All-America Selection Rose Display Garden near Cinderella Castle and a collection of Old World roses at United Kingdom in Epcot. At Disneyland, hundreds of showy floribunda roses greet guests at the park entrance. Elsewhere, miniature roses add to the Victorian charm of Main Street, U.S.A., and clusters of polyantha roses billow dreamily at Snow White's Grotto, near Sleeping Beauty Castle.

A rose may be a rose, but a rose properly planted, fertilized, fed and watered is healthy one. Some tips:

PLANTING

- Choose a location that receives at least five hours of sunlight a day.

- Make sure the area has good air circulation so that leaves stay dry to reduce the risk of fungus.

- Check the drainage of the area—roses don't like wet feet.

- Dig the hole a little bigger than the rootball and add organic matter to encourage root growth.

- Roses can be planted to the depth of the bud union.

- Gently push the soil around the roots to eliminate air pockets, continuing to add soil until the hole is three-quarters full.

1

- Fill the hole with water; let it soak, then fill again.

- After the water has soaked in, readjust the rose if necessary and continue filling with soil.

- Water in the morning so the foliage can dry.

- Give roses an inch of water a week.

FEEDING

- Regular fertilization is a must. Feed roses with a granular slow-release fertilizer at least three times a year.

- Before fertilizing, pull back mulch from around the stem.

- Apply fertilizer in the spring right after pruning.

- Reapply fertilizer just after flower buds develop.

- Fertilize again two to three months before the first frost.

PRUNING

- Hard prune roses every year in early spring as the buds begin to swell—leave about four of the strongest canes and prune about two feet up from the ground.

- If pruning for a bush shape, clip crossover branches from the center to promote a stronger bush.

- Pruning the bush about fifteen inches off the ground into an open cup shape will promote air flow and reduce vulnerability to disease.

- Prune damaged and diseased branches to just below the problem area.

- Roses that bloom on the previous year's growth, such as old-fashioneds and climbers, should be pruned right after flowering.

The Osteospermum hybrid "Lemon Symphony," a daisy developed by Proven Winners plant brand, features stunning yellow flowers with uncommon violet eyes. Heat tolerant and prolific, the beauties make music at Walt Disney World from summer through fall.

photo credits